For Mom and Pops, who always found a way – C.R.

To my amazingly awesome daughter, Allister,
and to Katrin for all of her help – M.L.

Bloomsbury Publishing, London, Berlin, New York and Sydney

First published in Great Britain in February 2011 by Bloomsbury Publishing Plc
36 Soho Square, London, W1D 3QY

Text copyright © Candace Ryan 2011
Illustrations copyright © Mike Lowery 2011
The moral right of the author and illustrator has been asserted

Text hand-lettered by Mike Lowery

A CIP catalogue record of this book is available from the British Library

ISBN 978 1 4088 1441 3

Printed in China by C & C Offset Co Ltd, Shenzhen, Guangdong

1 3 5 7 9 10 8 6 4 2

www.bloomsbury.com

RIBBIT RABBIT

CANDACE RYAN

illustrated by
MIKE LOWERY

BLOOMSBURY
LONDON BERLIN NEW YORK SYDNEY

FROG AND BUNNY
ARE {BEST} FRIENDS.

RIBBIT RABBIT.
RABBIT RIBBIT.

THEY EVEN EAT
PEANUT-BUTTER
SANDWICHES TOGETHER.

BUT THEY DON'T ALWAYS GET ALONG.

SOMETIMES THEY FIGHT OVER LITTLE THINGS.

RIBBIT RABBIT.

NIP IT,

SOMETIMES THEY FIGHT OVER

BIG

THINGS...

RIBBIT RABBIT.

TRIP IT,

...UNTIL EVERY :BIG:

AND (LITTLE) THING

MAKES THEM FIGHT.

RIBBIT RABBIT.

YIP IT,

AND THEY FIND
THEMSELVES ALL
ALONE.

RIBBIT RABBIT.

"

FLIP IT,

FLAP IT.

THEN, FROG THINKS
ABOUT BUNNY,
AND BUNNY THINKS
ABOUT FROG.

RIBBIT
RABBIT.

TIP IT,

TAP IT.

THEY KNOW WHAT THEY HAVE TO DO...

RIBBIT RABBIT.

GRIP IT,

GRAB IT.

AND WHEN THEY COME
BACK TOGETHER AGAIN...

**RIBBIT
RABBIT.**

**RABBIT
RIBBIT.**